Monkey in the Story Tree

I see a monkey in the tree.

He writes letters a b c!

He writes words cat dog run.

4

I see a monkey having fun!

A big dog runs after a little cat.

The cat runs and runs.

I see his story. I see his art.

The cat runs
up the tree.

The cat is
in the tree
with me.

That little monkey is very smart!

7

1. Look for five words from the story. Write the words.

2. Use those words and other words to write your own story.

I was walking on the beach.

I saw something shiny. It was a box.

A little fish jumped out.

"Thank you for letting me go."